Printed in the United States of America
First Edition
1 3 5 7 9 10 8 6 4 2
V475-2873-0-12214
Library of Congress Control Number 2012934137
ISBN 978-1-4231-6702-2
For more Disney Press fun, visit www.disneybooks.com

Adapted by Catherine Hapka

Based on characters created by Robert Vince and Anna McRoberts

Santa Paws 2: The Santa Pups is based on the screenplay written by Robert Vince and Anna McRoberts

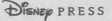

DISNEP PRESS

New York

The North Pole

Six Months Before Christmas

It was a beautiful, snowy July day at the North Pole. Suddenly, a door crashed open in Santa's Workshop. Santa Claus burst in.

"The Santa Pups are coming!" he cried.

Santa rushed to his house. His head elf, Eli, followed. So did Eddy, Santa's head elf dog.

The magnificent snow-white dog known as Santa Paws paced nervously outside Santa Claus's bedroom door. Inside, Mrs. Claus was helping Mrs. Paws have her puppies. Eli went in, too. Finally Mrs. Claus emerged.

"The Santa Pups have arrived," she told Santa Paws. "You have three beautiful daughters and a son."

"Congratulations, old friend," Santa Claus said.

"I can't believe it!" Santa Paws exclaimed. "I'm a father!"

Mrs. Claus smiled. "Let's go in and meet the puppies, shall we?"

In the bedroom, Mrs. Paws looked tired but happy. "Aren't they adorable?" she said.

"What are you going to name the little darlings?" Mrs. Claus asked.

Mrs. Paws had been thinking about names for months. But as she looked from one pup to the next, she saw that they could practically name themselves. One had a musical voice, and seemed to sing instead of speak. She would be called Jingle. Another was yipping and licking the others. She was to be called Charity. The third girl was the smallest of the litter, and her name became Hope.

Finally, there was the little boy pup. "He's bound to take after his dad," Santa Paws said. "Strong, good looking, great leader . . ."

"Don't forget modest," Mrs. Paws added with a smile.

"That too," Santa Paws agreed. "I was thinking that Noble would be a fitting name."

Mrs. Paws, Mrs. Claus, and Santa Claus all smiled. It was perfect.

And so the Santa Pups were born and named.

Chapter One

Five Months Later

It was three weeks until Christmas, and Santa's Workshop was busy, busy, busy. Eli and the other elves, and Eddy and the elf dogs were hard at work making toys.

The Santa Pups were bigger now. They loved running and playing in the workshop. Sometimes they loved it a little *too* much.

Jingle was always singing, but she

was still learning to find the right notes. That meant she usually found the *wrong* ones. Listening to her was hard on the elves' sensitive ears.

Hope was still the smallest of the Pups. She lived up to her name, just like Jingle. She was always so hopeful everything would work out that she never looked before she leaped. And when she leaped into the middle of a box of ribbons or a table of unfinished toys, it caused *big* problems.

Then there was Charity. She didn't seem to understand the meaning of her name yet, because she wasn't very good at sharing. She growled whenever the other Pups tried to take one of her bones.

Noble had made himself leader of the Pups. That most often meant leading his sisters—and himself—straight into trouble.

On this particular day, the Pups were causing even more chaos in the workshop than usual. Finally, their father had had enough.

"Hope, Jingle, Charity, Noble!" Santa Paws yelled. "I suggest you go with Eddy and Eli to school. Now!"

"Yes, Dad," the Pups replied in unison.

Soon all four of the puppies were sitting in front of a magical chalkboard. Eli was talking. And talking. And talking.

"And that leads us to the most important lesson of all about our very precious magic crystals," he explained, pointing to a diagram on the chalkboard. "Only Santa Claus, Mrs. Claus, Santa Paws, Mrs. Paws, Comet, Eddy, and yours truly"—he pointed to himself—"have magic crystals. They are what we use to make the magic of Christmas happen."

Eddy came in. He glanced at the Pups to see if they were paying attention.

They weren't. All four of the Pups were sound asleep at their desks.

"Um, Eli," Eddy said, "I think you've lost your audience."

Eli finally noticed the snoozing Pups. "Santa Pups!" he exclaimed, annoyed. "This is a very important lesson about the magic crystals!"

The Pups woke up. "Maybe we'd pay closer attention if we had our own crystals," Noble said. The crystals would allow them to do cool Christmas magic!

"Magic crystals have great power and with great power comes great responsibility," Eli said. "You don't *get* a magic crystal, you *earn* a magic crystal."

"Can I earn one by singing?" Jingle asked. She cleared her throat and sang loudly: *"Hark the herald Jingle sings—"*

"Not exactly," Eli said, cutting her off. "Magic crystals are earned when one understands the true meaning of Christmas and is ready to use Christmas magic to do good deeds and grant Christmas wishes around the world."

"Are you serious?" Noble exclaimed. "Good Deed is my middle name!"

"And we'd be extremely good at

granting Christmas wishes," Hope added.

"You Pups are far from ready to grant wishes," Eddy said, shaking his head. "You must have a much better understanding of what Christmas really is before that day comes."

"We've learned everything about Christmas," Hope protested.

Eddy shook his head. "You Pups hardly know anything about the greatest day there is!"

"That's not true," Charity said. "We know about wishes, toys, and how much I love getting presents!"

"And how fast Santa's sleigh can go!" Hope chimed in. "And how we're not supposed to be in it, even if we're just pretending to drive."

"That's the easy stuff," Eddy said. "It's not the true Spirit of Christmas."

Eddy tried to continue the lessons. But Noble had another question. "What makes the crystals magic to begin with?" he asked.

Eddy smiled. "Why, that's a very good question," he said. "And one that just might require a field trip."

"Field trip!" all the Pups cheered. "Woo-hoo!"

Soon Eli, Eddy, and the Santa Pups were in a cave staring up at a huge, glowing icicle.

"This right here, Pups, is the heart of all Christmas magic," Eli began. He went on to explain that the Great Christmas Icicle supplied all the energy to make

Christmas happen. It powered the workshop, made Santa's sleigh fly, and created the magic in the crystals.

"So where does the energy in the Great Christmas Icicle come from, you ask?" Eli continued. "Well, that's where the Great Spirit Map comes in. . . ."

Eli and Eddy led the Pups back to the workshop. On the wall was a large map of the world covered with glowing dots. The dots were all different colors, some brighter than others.

"As you can see, Pups," Eli said, "the Spirit Map allows us to monitor Christmas Spirit as it comes in from all over the world." He looked toward an elf who was working in front of the map. "Zoom in on Pineville, Elpert."

An elf named Elpert moved a magnifying glass to a large red dot in Montana. The dot pulsed more brightly than anything else on the map.

Santa Paws was working nearby. He glanced over at the map and smiled.

"Pineville is the number one town for emitting Christmas Spirit," he said.

Santa Claus nodded. "Christmas Spirit is contagious. A town like Pineville can have an impact far beyond the town itself. The greater the Christmas Spirit, the more energy the Great Christmas Icicle will have.

"And the better the magic crystals will work!" Noble said.

"Very good, Noble," Eli replied with a nod.

"So now can we have our own crystals?" Noble asked.

Eli gave the puppy a stern look.

Nearby, Santa Paws was motioning to the map. "We have to give credit to our ambassadors to the Santa Cause," he said. "They ensure that Christmas Spirit is maintained all year long. There must be a really special ambassador in Pineville."

Mrs. Claus sighed sadly. "Unfortunately, we recently lost one of our best ambassadors in Pineville," she said. "If we don't replace the ambassador soon, Christmas Spirit may start to decrease."

"I had no idea!" Santa Claus exclaimed. "This is a serious matter that needs our attention. But with Christmas three weeks away, I can't leave the workshop."

"I could go," Mrs. Claus suggested. "Someone has to."

Santa Claus agreed. He asked Eli and the other elves to prepare the sleigh to leave that very day so Mrs. Claus could go to Pineville. Everyone rushed off in different directions.

Everyone except the Pups, that is.

"Hey, Pups, I've got a Santa Pups plan!" Noble whispered to his sisters. "We're going to take Eddy's crystal, fly to Pineville with Mrs. Claus, and grant as many Christmas wishes as we can. Then Eli and Eddy will see that we're ready for crystals of our own!"

"Do we even know how to grant a Christmas wish?" Hope wondered.

"We'll figure it out," Noble told her with a shrug.

Charity shook her head. "Noble, even *I* know that stealing is the opposite of giving."

"We'll just borrow the crystal," Noble explained. "Besides, how would we grant wishes without one?"

His sisters didn't have an answer for that. So they all agreed to the plan.

Noble grinned. "Pineville, USA, here we come!"

Chapter Two

The townspeople of Pineville, USA, were busy decorating for Christmas. Every building had signs of holiday cheer—from the bank to the town hall to the butcher shop. The church bell rang merrily as a light snowfall dusted everything with sparkling flakes.

Mayor Denny happily strolled along Main Street, smiling and greeting the townspeople. He loved Christmas. Then again, *everyone* in Pineville loved Christmas!

Well, almost everyone. A boy named Carter Reynolds was riding his bike along Main Street. But he wasn't looking at the decorations or humming along with the songs the other townsfolk were singing. He wasn't even smiling.

He stopped his bike in front of the town radio station, 87.9 XMAS-FM. The radio tower twinkled with hundreds of Christmas lights, but Carter barely spared it a glance.

When he went inside, his father and sister were in the control booth. Both of them looked joyful.

"There you are, Carter!" Mr. Reynolds

said to his son. "You missed the lighting up of the radio station."

Carter's seven-year-old sister, Sarah, nodded. "We were going to let you turn on the lights. It's your favorite part."

"That's okay, Sarah," Carter said. "I don't care about Christmas anymore."

Sarah looked at her brother with wide eyes. "Don't say that, Carter."

"What's the big deal about it anyway?" Carter replied, though he saw the sad look on his sister's face. "It's just another holiday."

Mr. Reynolds looked at Carter with concern. "He's just tired, Sarah. Aren't you, buddy? We should get home," he told both kids. "Uncle Jeb and Mayor Denny are joining us for dinner."

They hurried home, arriving shortly before their guests. Along with the mayor, Mr. Reynolds had invited the kids' uncle, Jeb Gibson, who ran the Pineville Animal Shelter. Jeb had brought his loyal dog, Baxter, as well.

Mr. Reynolds was glad to have friends for dinner with his family. The dining table seemed too big for just the three of them these days.

Sarah volunteered to say grace before they ate. "Thank you for this food and for Christmas, the most wonderful time of the year," she said. "And thank you for my big brother, Carter. And please say hello to our mommy for us. Please tell her we miss her very much and are thinking of her always and always. Amen."

The mayor could see that Mr. Reynolds and Carter both looked sad. He decided to change the subject.

"How are things at the animal shelter, Jeb?" he asked.

Jeb dug into his meat loaf. "Well, we have a few more dogs to find homes for before Christmas. But Baxter and I will get it done. We always like to have an empty shelter because it means everyone's found a home." He smiled down at his dog and then looked up at the kids. "Tell me about what you have planned for Christmas."

"I'm going to help Daddy put on the Christmas show at the radio station," Sarah said eagerly. "I'm going to sing on Christmas Eve, just like Mommy used to."

"That's music to my ears, Sarah," Mayor Denny said. "The radio station has been keeping the Christmas Spirit alive for the people of Pineville ever since your mother was your age."

"Dad, may I be excused?" Carter broke in.

"You haven't eaten anything," Mr. Reynolds pointed out.

Carter stood up, not looking at anyone. "I'm just not hungry." He hurried upstairs.

Jeb looked worried. "How's he holding up, Tom?" he asked.

Mr. Reynolds shook his head. "It's been hard on him." He paused. "It's been hard on all of us."

"Any luck finding a nanny?" Jeb asked.

"Not yet," Mr. Reynolds said. "I just

put the ad in the newspaper yesterday."

Jeb nodded and patted his brother on the back. Then they all quietly ate their dinner.

Chapter Three

Back at Santa's Workshop, Mrs. Claus was almost ready to depart. Santa, Eli, and a couple of other elves watched her climb into the sleigh.

"I'll be back in a Christmas minute," Mrs. Claus promised.

"Don't worry, Santa," added Comet, a reindeer. "We'll take good care of her."

Mrs. Claus picked up the reins. The reindeers' hooves began to glow, and the sleigh lifted off the ground and flew into the sky. A moment later, a puppy face peeked out of the back.

"Guys," Noble whispered to his sisters, "I think we're airborne!"

It was a long flight to Pineville. The Pups spent most of the trip sleeping or peeking out at the scenery passing by far beneath the sleigh. Mrs. Claus and the reindeer never noticed the stowaways. Finally the sleigh reached its destination.

The reindeer swooped down and landed in a field. Mrs. Claus noticed that there was a big, beautiful old barn on the property. And it was empty.

"Why don't you spend a few days here," she told the reindeer.

The reindeer pulled the sleigh inside. "Good idea, Mrs. C," Comet said. "We're pooped."

A reindeer named Dancer nodded. "Those headwinds were tough."

Mrs. Claus smiled at the reindeer and left the barn. She made her way to town and wandered down Main Street. Christmas music was playing over the town's speakers. Every building glittered with Christmas lights. Everywhere she looked, people were smiling at one another. She watched a boy rush to help an elderly woman cross the street.

"This town certainly has an abundance

of Christmas Spirit," Mrs. Claus murmured to herself.

She couldn't wait to find the next Christmas ambassador!

Meanwhile, back at the farm, the reindeer lay down for a rest. Soon the old barn was quiet.

Noble poked his head out of the sleigh and looked around. "Okay, Pups," he whispered. "Time to make our move, but we've got to be completely silent."

"*Silent night . . .*" Jingle sang.

Noble sighed. "That's not exactly what I meant. Come on!"

The Santa Pups climbed down from the sleigh and tiptoed out of the barn. They heard shouts of laughter from nearby. The Pups followed the sound to a frozen pond, where kids were skating while their parents chatted on the bank.

Two ten-year-old girls were helping their friend learn to skate. The girl's legs wobbled as her friends held her up on the ice.

"I wish I could skate really well," she told the other girls.

The Santa Pups were listening. "Did you hear that?" Noble asked his sisters. "Time to grant our first Christmas wish!"

"Yes!" Hope said. "Let's go for it!"

Noble closed his eyes to focus. The crystal on Eddy's collar began to glow, and magic energy surrounded the girl.

A second later, the girl sped up. Her feet skimmed confidently across the ice. Then she leaped and spun in the air.

Her friends' eyes widened. "How'd you do that?" they asked.

"I have no idea!" the girl exclaimed.

"This is going to be even easier than I thought!" Noble whispered as the Pups watched.

Jingle nodded. "Let's do it again!"

Chapter Four

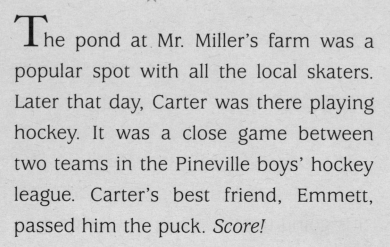

The pond at Mr. Miller's farm was a popular spot with all the local skaters. Later that day, Carter was there playing hockey. It was a close game between two teams in the Pineville boys' hockey league. Carter's best friend, Emmett, passed him the puck. *Score!*

A whistle blew. "That's the game, kids!" called Mr. Miller. "Final score is

Blue Jackets 3, Meteors 2."

Mr. Miller was their referee and coach. He let the teams practice and play on the frozen pond all the time.

"Okay, gather around," he said as the players skated off the ice. He gestured to a dozen wagons and wheelbarrows parked in the snow nearby. "I see you all brought your wagons. Just like every year, you guys should collect gifts from around town so I can take them to the orphanage. We need to make sure that those less fortunate boys and girls have a nice Christmas, too."

As the boys scattered, Carter grabbed a wagon and walked along beside Emmett. "It's going to take hours to fill this darn Christmas wagon," he complained.

"I like doing the Christmas wagon,"

Emmett replied. "It's like being Santa Claus for a day."

Carter didn't answer. Who cared about Santa Claus? He was ready for the whole Christmas season to be over.

The two boys headed toward town.

The Santa Pups had found their way to town, too. They were all very impressed by the festive Christmas decorations in Pineville's shops. They stopped to admire the Santa display in the window of the hardware store, then moved on to the toy store.

A little boy and girl stood staring in the window. "I hope Santa brings me that train set," the boy said.

His sister was missing her two front

teeth. When she spoke, the *s* sounds came out like a whistle.

"All I want for Chrissstmasss isss my two front teeth ssso I don't sssound ssso sssilly," she said. "I'm ssssick of everyone teassssing me at ssssschool and calling me ssssilly Sssally."

"That poor girl," Jingle whispered to the other Pups. "If I was missing my two front teeth, imagine how bad my singing would sound!"

"Now *that* is a totally scary thought," Charity agreed.

"Watch this, Pups!" Noble whispered. "I wish that girl had her two front teeth!"

The crystal glowed. Magic dust drifted toward the girl's face, and her teeth grew in lickety-split!

"Whoa!" her brother cried. "Your teeth!"

The girl felt her new teeth with her fingers. "Let's go show Mom!"

Noble smiled as the kids raced off. "This is easy!" he told the other Pups. "I knew we were ready for crystals of our own."

Hope agreed. "I could do this all day long!"

Chapter Five

"That was 'Deck the Halls,'" Mr. Reynolds said into the microphone. He glanced at Sarah, who was sitting next to him at the radio station. "And now, a real treat and a preview of our Christmas special. Many of you will recognize this song from my late wife, Michelle. Sung now for the first time by our daughter, Sarah Reynolds."

He lowered the microphone to Sarah's height. Sarah leaned forward and began to sing a song called "My Blue Christmas."

Her voice was beautiful and pure as she sang about missing someone special at Christmastime. All over town, people stopped to listen.

Mrs. Claus was one of those people. She stopped short outside a dress shop. The shop's owners were three sisters named Agnes, Dorothy, and Blue Bright. They came outside to listen and saw Mrs. Claus standing there.

"Isn't her singing magical?" Blue asked.

"It most certainly is," Mrs. Claus replied.

She looked around. Everyone on the

street was listening to the song. There wasn't a dry eye to be seen.

"That's it," Mrs. Claus whispered to herself as the song ended. "It's her! She must be the reason I'm here."

"What's that?" Agnes asked.

"Nothing," Mrs. Claus said. "Please, excuse me, but could you tell me who was singing?"

"Why, that's little Sarah Reynolds," Dorothy replied.

Blue nodded. "Her mother ran the radio station and used to sing each Christmas for the town. But she fell ill and passed this fall."

"The whole town was so sad," Agnes said. "And that poor family was devastated."

"But little Sarah, well, she just stepped right in and took over," Dorothy added.

"You could say she's Pineville's little Christmas miracle," Blue finished.

"I see," Mrs. Claus said. "I must meet this young lady!"

The Brights pointed toward the radio station. Mrs. Claus thanked them, then realized she hadn't introduced herself.

"I'm Mrs. . . ." She paused, realizing she couldn't give her real name. She glanced around and spotted a candy cane decorating a nearby window. "Er, Cane," she said. "Mrs. Cane. Good-bye for now, and Merry Christmas!"

Then she hurried off toward the radio station. It was easy to find, since it had so many beautiful decorations.

"Merry Christmas!" Sarah said when Mrs. Claus walked in. "Can I help you?"

"Are you the little girl who was singing that beautiful song just now?" When Sarah nodded, Mrs. Claus smiled. "You were wonderful! Who taught you to sing like that?"

"My mommy," Sarah said. "She sings with the angels now."

"It sounds to me like she passed the Christmas Spirit on to you," Mrs. Claus said.

Sarah smiled. "Every year she did the Christmas radio show. We're doing it again this year, but without her."

"I bet you will make it very magical," Mrs. Claus said.

Mr. Reynolds was at the desk nearby

looking at the station's bills. He glanced up and noticed Mrs. Claus.

"How can we help you?" he asked politely. Then he smiled. "Oh! You must be here for the nanny position!"

Mrs. Claus was thrilled that she'd found her new Christmas ambassador. "Oh, I'm sorry to disappoint you—" she began.

Mr. Reynolds didn't let her finish. "I'm looking for someone to help me with the kids while I'm at my real job. Actually, I'm a lawyer, but from now until Christmas I'm going to be here at the station full-time trying to keep the show going."

Sarah smiled up at the confused Mrs. Claus. "Will you be my nanny? I have a feeling I'd like you very much."

"Aren't you sweet," Mrs. Claus said. "But as I was trying to explain, Mister, er—"

"Reynolds," Mr. Reynolds finished. "Thomas Reynolds. And this is Sarah. Have you been working with children long?"

"I suppose you could say all my life," Mrs. Claus replied. "But as I was trying to say—"

"Pineville's a pretty small place," Mr. Reynolds interrupted again. "We know everyone. You must be from out of town?"

"Indeed I am, from up north."

"Tell you what," Mr. Reynolds said. "Don't say anything—I want you to think about this. Why don't you come over for dinner? You can meet my son, Carter, and we can all discuss this over my world-famous meat loaf."

Sarah reached for Mrs. Claus's hand. "Yes, please come over for dinner!"

Mrs. Claus melted when she looked at Sarah's sweet smile. How could she resist a child's sincere wish?

"I suppose a nice, warm meal would do me good," she said. "I accept."

Chapter Six

The sun had set, and the air was growing chilly on Main Street. Most of the shops had long since closed for the evening.

Carter and Emmett were still pulling their wagon. The Santa Pups watched them.

"Those boys look like they could use some help," Charity said.

Carter didn't notice the Pups. "I'm wiped out and starving," he complained to Emmett. "Let's call it a night."

Emmett glanced at their wagon and nodded. He didn't think the wagon could hold much more anyway.

They pulled the wagon up over the curb. *BUMP-THUMP!* It tipped over, spilling gifts all around.

That was the last straw for Carter. "This is so stupid!" he cried. "I'm sick and tired of all this Christmas stuff!"

"You shouldn't think that way, Carter." Emmett bent to grab the spilled gifts, stacking them back in the wagon. "Those kids at the orphanage don't have parents to get them presents. They should have a chance to be happy, too."

The Pups were still watching. But they were too far away to hear everything clearly.

"What are they saying?" Jingle wondered.

"Something about being happy," Hope said.

"That sounds good," Charity decided.

"Come on, Pups," said Noble. "If there's a wish here, we should grant it!"

He closed his eyes and concentrated. The magic crystal around his neck started to glow.

Carter was glaring at his friend, feeling more frustrated than ever. Why couldn't anyone understand how he felt? All they could talk about was Christmas, Christmas, Christmas . . . and Carter knew that Christmas would never be the same again.

"I wish all this Christmas Spirit would just go away!" he blurted out angrily.

"Wait!" Jingle exclaimed as magic dust drifted toward Carter. "Stop! Noble! Don't grant that wish!"

But it was too late. A cold winter wind gusted through the town. The lights flickered. Many of the colorful Christmas lights decorating the streets and shops started to burst. *Pop! Pop! Pop!*

A cloud of dust swirled around Carter and Emmett. Carter closed his eyes and sighed. He already felt bad about what he'd said. It was just that everything about Christmas reminded him of his mother. . . .

"Look, Emmett, I'm sorry," he said. "I shouldn't have blown up at you like that."

"Don't worry about it." Emmett had his back to Carter. "I mean, you're right, Christmas is pretty ridiculous when you think about it."

Carter was surprised by his friend's sudden change in attitude. "Well, yeah, I guess," he said. "Come on, let's get this wagon thing over with."

Emmett turned around. His whole expression had changed. Instead of his usual cheery smile, he looked angry.

"You know what?" he said. "I'm going to head home."

"But I can't pull the wagon by myself," Carter protested. He wondered if Emmett was joking around.

But Emmett didn't crack a smile. "Whatever." He shrugged. "Just leave it, then. We'll tell Mr. Miller we were robbed or something. Unless we want to keep all the stuff for ourselves."

"What are you saying?" Carter exclaimed. "We can't take toys from orphans!"

Emmett shrugged and turned away. "See ya."

"Emmett, where are you going?" Carter called after his friend. "Emmett?"

"What do we do?" Jingle asked nervously.

Noble gulped. "I think we made a very big mistake, Pups," he said. "And Eddy never told us how to reverse a wish."

"That's because Eddy said we weren't

ready for our own crystals, *remember*?" Charity replied, giving her brother a stern look.

"Why did I let you guys talk me into all this?" Noble groaned.

Charity glared at him. "Seriously, I hope you're kidding!"

Chapter Seven

Carter was huffing and puffing by the time he reached the coffee shop. Jeb's truck was parked outside.

Leaving the wagon by the door, Carter hurried into the shop. A rush of wind blew a cloud of dust in with him, and the lights flickered. But Carter didn't notice. He was focused on Jeb, who was sitting at the counter eating pie and chatting with the waitress. Baxter wagged his tail as Carter hurried over.

"Uncle Jeb!" Carter exclaimed. "Am I ever glad to see you!"

Jeb smiled at him. "Hey, Carter. What's up, my boy?"

"It's this wagon." Carter gestured toward the wagon full of gifts. "I need to pull it all the way to Mr. Miller's house tonight so he can deliver the presents to the orphans, but it's too heavy and Emmett was helping me but he totally flipped out. . . ."

Just then, the dust reached Jeb. It swirled around him, and suddenly his friendly expression started to change.

Carter didn't notice at first. "Can you give me and the wagon a ride?" he asked. Then he peered at Jeb, wondering why his uncle was frowning all of a sudden.

"Look, I'm way too busy to help you, can't you see?" Jeb responded harshly.

Carter was surprised and a little hurt. He turned and left.

The Pups watched as Carter tried to pull the wagon by himself.

"We have to find a way to reverse this wish!" Noble said.

Jingle nodded. "We'd better find Mrs. Claus. She'll know what to do."

"The boy is leaving," Hope reminded them. "We can't lose him until we fix this!"

"Hope's totally right," Charity agreed. "We can't let him get away."

They started to follow Carter. But Jeb

had just emerged from the coffee shop and spotted them.

"I've never seen those pups before," he said, his eyed narrowed.

Baxter saw the puppies, too. "I haven't seen you pups before," he barked to them. "Are you new in town?"

"We're the Santa Pups from the North Pole," Noble replied. "I'm Noble, and these are my sisters, Hope, Jingle, and Charity."

Baxter was impressed. "Is your father Santa Paws?"

"Yes!" Hope cried. "Do you know our dad?"

"All dogs know about Santa Paws," Baxter replied. "Christmas is my favorite time of year. In Pineville, it's everyone's favorite time of year."

Jeb kneeled down beside the Pups. He had a sly smile on his face.

"What do we have here?" he asked. He offered the Pups a treat.

"Yuck," Noble said when he tried the doggy treat. "What is that? You wouldn't happen to have a candy cane, would you?"

Jeb frowned. "Let's put a lid on all this barking," he snapped.

"I'm not barking, I'm talking," Noble replied.

"Oh, no!" Jingle realized what was happening. "He can't understand us!"

Charity nodded. "Remember? Eddy taught us that people can only understand North Pole animals if they truly believe in Christmas. He must not believe!"

"Don't worry, Pups," Baxter said. "My human is just trying to help you."

Meanwhile, Jeb had noticed the crystal on Noble's collar. "That's quite the little sparkler you have there," he remarked. "I'm going to have to confiscate this."

"You can't take that!" Charity protested. "We have to give it back to Eddy!"

But Jeb yanked the collar off Noble's neck. Then he grabbed the Pups.

"It seems it'll be Christmas in the pound for you," he snarled.

Baxter looked shocked. "What's going on here?"

At the North Pole, Santa Claus and the elves were hard at work when the lights suddenly flickered. Santa glanced up, surprised by the interruption in the energy from the Great Christmas Icicle.

Eddy raced into the room. "My crystal collar is missing!" he exclaimed. "At first I thought Ellis and Elpert were playing one of their elf pranks. But it's definitely gone!"

"We would never play an elf prank with your magic crystal," Elpert said seriously.

Santa was concerned. A missing crystal was an important matter indeed. He glanced at the Spirit Map.

"Let's do a location search on Eddy's crystal," he said.

"You got it, Santa," Ellis responded. The Spirit Map zoomed in.

"There it is!" Eli cried, pointing. "Right in the heart of Pineville."

Then Santa Paws came in, looking worried. "Has anyone seen the Santa Pups?" he asked. "They're taking mischief to a whole new level today. We can't find them anywhere. Their mother's getting worried."

Eddy shook his head. "My *professional* guesstimation is those rascals decided to 'borrow' my crystal and then hitch a sleigh ride to Pineville with Mrs. Claus."

Santa Claus smiled. "I'm sure Mrs. Claus has everything under control."

Santa Paws sighed, still looking worried. "I hope they're okay—and not causing any trouble down there."

Chapter Eight

Carter was exhausted by the time he got home. When he came in, his father and sister were sitting with Mrs. Claus near the undecorated Christmas tree.

"Oh, here's Carter now. Hey, you missed dinner," Mr. Reynolds said gently to his son. "We were worried about you. Say hello to Mrs. Cane. We're hoping she'll be our new nanny."

Mrs. Claus smiled. "Hello, Carter."

Mr. Reynolds peered at his son. "What's up, Carter? You look beat."

"First, Emmett loses it," Carter said with a sigh. "Then Uncle Jeb wouldn't help me, and I had to drag the wagon full of toys to Mr. Miller's barn by myself."

"Well, why don't we get some of my world-famous meat loaf in you," Mr. Reynolds suggested. "Then we can all decorate the tree. That'll brighten your mood."

"Dad, I'm too beat to help with the tree," Carter said wearily. "Can you guys just do it without me?"

Just then, a puff of wind gusted through the house, blowing a cloud of dust around Mr. Reynolds. His happy expression turned gloomy.

"Yeah, sure," he said. "To be honest, I'm a little tired. And it's pretty late."

Carter was surprised. It wasn't like his dad to give up so easily.

Sarah was surprised, too. "But you said we were going to decorate the tree tonight," she reminded him.

"It's just a tree. It'll still be here tomorrow," Mr. Reynolds said. "Why don't you go on up to bed."

Sarah was disappointed. But she didn't want to complain if her father was tired. Instead, she begged him to let Mrs. Cane stay overnight in their guest room.

Mr. Reynolds shrugged, not seeming

All of the helpers in Santa's Workshop are getting ready for Christmas.

The Santa Pups have to learn the meaning of Christmas before they can earn their own magic crystals.

Noble grabs a magic crystal. The Santa Pups are
going to Pineville to prove themselves!

Once the coast is clear, the Santa Pups check out
where they've landed!

They're at Mr. Miller's farm, where the boys'
ice hockey team uses his pond for practice.

The Santa Pups explore the town of Pineville.

The radio station is festively decorated by the Reynolds family.

Suddenly, Baxter notices that the people of Pineville seem to have lost their Christmas Spirit.

The Santa Pups are thrown in the pound! They've caused Pineville's spirit to go away *and* lost their magic crystal. They have to get out!

At the North Pole, the elves realize that something is wrong in Pineville. They create a magical ice cream truck to take Eli and Eddy there.

Baxter frees the Santa Pups from their cage!

Eddy lands in Pineville. He must stop the town's Christmas Spirit from dropping any more.

The Santa Pups go find their magic crystal. Brutis guards the pawn shop but lets the Pups pass.

The Santa Pups and Baxter look for Mrs. Claus—they need her!

With the help of Sarah and Carter Reynolds,
Christmas Spirit is saved!

The Santa Pups wish everyone a merry Christmas!

to care one way or the other. "There's enough space."

Sarah gave Mrs. Claus a tour of the house, including her room and her favorite photo of her mother. But she couldn't stop thinking about something.

"Mrs. Cane?" she said. "I'm worried. Carter doesn't want to do anything for Christmas."

"Well, he's just a little under the weather right now," Mrs. Claus told her. "I think he has a little Christmas cold."

"A Christmas cold? How do we make it better?" Sarah asked.

"Just like with any other cold, you must help them through it," Mrs. Claus explained. "But a Christmas cold is special, and it takes a special kind of treatment to make it better."

"Like what?" Sarah asked.

Mrs. Claus told her that the cure for Christmas colds was to spread Christmas cheer to everyone.

"You're not really a nanny, are you?" Sarah asked with a yawn.

Mrs. Claus tucked her in bed. "No dear, I'm not," she said with a smile.

Chapter Nine

Jeb was in a bad mood as he dragged the Santa Pups into the animal shelter. It was a cheery place, with toys and comfortable beds for each animal and not a cage to be seen. There were only a few dogs sleeping in the cozy room.

As he looked around, Jeb frowned. Why did a bunch of mutts need to be so comfortable, anyway? He was ready to change a lot of things around here.

Grabbing a large cage from the storage area, he shoved the Pups inside. "In the cage," he snarled.

"Well, guys, this is my place," Baxter said. "Three meals a day, doggy toys, rubber balls." Suddenly he noticed what Jeb was doing. "Uh, why are you putting them in the cage? You never put anyone in the cage."

"Quit your barking, Baxter," Jeb yelled at his dog. "And, you stay out of the way or you'll be joining them, you hear me?"

Baxter backed off, surprised by how mean Jeb was acting. He watched as Jeb locked the cage and stormed out.

"I'm sorry, Pups," Baxter said. "This has never happened before. He's usually very nice. I don't know what's gotten into him."

"You have to help us," Charity said. "We came here to prove we're ready for our own magic crystals."

"But we made a very big mistake," Jingle added.

Noble nodded. "And if we don't get that collar back, Christmas could be in big trouble!"

At the North Pole, Santa Claus was staring at the Spirit Map. Santa Paws, Mrs. Paws, Eli, Eddy, Ellis, and Elpert were gathered around him.

"What could cause all that Christmas Spirit to just disappear?" Santa Claus wondered.

"Well, sir, you don't know the half of it," Eli told him. "We've all seen the effects of a Christmas cold,"

Eddy shuddered. "This is more like a Christmas flu!"

"The Christmas Spirit Multiplier Effect is working in reverse," Eli said. "Lack of Spirit is spreading out of Pineville and across the country."

"If we don't fix it, it will spread at an exponential rate," Ellis said.

"We'll have a Christmas pandemic the likes of which we've never seen!" Eli cried.

Santa Paws suddenly realized what this meant. "Christmas Spirit could disappear forever!"

Santa Claus nodded. "Eli, Eddy, get to

Pineville as fast as you can. Find Mrs. Claus and find those Pups. We've got to get to the bottom of this."

"We'll take care of it, sir!" Eli said. He and the head elf dog raced off to get ready. Ellis and Elpert came along to help. Using the E.L.F. compressor, they could change their vehicle into anything they wanted.

"Hey, boss," Elpert said. "The E.L.F. compressor is ready."

"Excellent," Eli said. "The question is, what kind of vehicle wouldn't draw *any* attention in Pineville in the middle of winter?"

"I know!" Eddy said. "Ice cream is cold and so is winter. It's like instant camouflage!" He pressed some buttons on the compressor, and the vehicle instantly changed into an old-fashioned ice cream truck.

"Snazzy!" Eli said.

And with that, they were off.

Chapter Ten

The next morning, Sarah came downstairs to find the dining room transformed. The tabletop was covered with a beautiful tablecloth, and on top of that was a breakfast of homemade muffins and waffles, fruit, bacon, eggs, and more.

"How did you do all of this?" Sarah exclaimed when she saw Mrs. Claus.

Mrs. Claus smiled. "Its quite simple, really."

Sarah glanced at the living room, where the undecorated tree still stood sadly in the corner. "I wish we had decorated the tree," she said.

"Well, close your eyes and make a Christmas wish," Mrs. Claus told her with a wink.

Sarah closed her eyes. "I wish the tree was decorated like Mommy always did it."

The crystal around Mrs. Claus's neck glowed, and magic dust flew through the room. When Sarah opened her eyes, she gasped.

"Wow!" she cried, staring at the tree, which was now beautifully decorated. "It's exactly the same!"

Sarah was happily digging into her breakfast when her father wandered in, looking sleepy. He stared at all the food in surprise.

"How was your Yuletide rest, Mr. Reynolds?" Mrs. Claus asked.

"It was all right, I guess," Mr. Reynolds mumbled.

"Look, Daddy," Sarah said excitedly. "I decorated the Christmas tree."

"That's nice, Sarah," Mr. Reynolds said.

Sarah bit her lip. Her father didn't seem very excited. "Want to look closer?"

"I'm sorry, sweetie. Daddy's been really busy dealing with the radio station and all the work at the law firm." Mr. Reynolds sighed. "Frankly, all this

Christmas stuff has really worn me down."

He opened the newspaper. Sarah felt tears well up in her eyes as she glanced at Mrs. Claus. Did her father have a Christmas cold, too?

"Why don't you grab your things?" Mrs. Claus said gently. "I'll walk you to school."

When Sarah had left the room, Mrs. Claus turned to Mr. Reynolds. "But what about Sarah? She loves Christmas."

Mr. Reynolds sighed again. "Yeah, I know. But she's seven—and between you and me, don't you think she's a little old for all this 'Santa' stuff?"

Mrs. Claus was shocked. "You're never too old to believe in Christmas," she said.

The phone rang, and Mr. Reynolds answered it. Then Sarah returned with her backpack, and Mrs. Claus took her to school, as promised.

A short while later, the two of them were walking down Main Street. A dark cloud hung over the once sunny town.

Then Sarah spotted the life-size dancing Santa in the window of the hardware store. She stopped to gaze at it.

Mrs. Claus watched the dancing Santa figure with a smile. "It's a fine likeness of Mr. Claus," she commented.

At that moment a man named Owen hurried by. He slipped on a patch of icy snow in front of the hardware store and fell down.

The owner of the store, Mr. Kent, was shoveling the sidewalk. He dropped his shovel and rushed over. "Oh, my word, Owen?" he exclaimed. "Are you okay?"

Owen looked angry. "Why didn't you shovel your part of the sidewalk?" he yelled.

A puff of dust flew off him. Some of it landed on Mr. Kent, and his expression went dark.

"Why don't you watch where you're walking next time?" he yelled back.

Owen clenched his fist. "I'm going to sue you for all you're worth!"

Mr. Kent's only response was to go back inside and slam the door. Mrs. Claus and Sarah hurried to help Owen get up, but he waved them off.

"I can get up myself," he grumbled.

Sarah glanced over at the store window just in time to see the Santa stop dancing. Mr. Kent had unplugged it!

Mrs. Claus sighed. It looked as if the whole town had caught a Christmas cold overnight! "Come on, sweetheart," she said, leading Sarah away.

The two of them hurried down the street. When they reached the radio station, Sarah saw the mayor nailing something onto the front door.

"Hello, Mayor Denny," she said. "What are you doing?"

"I'm foreclosing on the building," Mayor Denny said. "Your father hasn't paid the rent in three months."

"But what about the fund-raiser they

have planned?" Mrs. Claus said. "I'm sure they'll make enough to pay."

"Ha!" Mayor Denny said. "Unlikely, given that there isn't even going to be a Christmas show."

"What do you mean?" Sarah cried.

"I spoke to your father this morning," the mayor said. "Seems he's given up on the radio station, too."

Sarah couldn't believe her ears. Had her dad really said that? "But Mom loved the radio station!" she exclaimed.

"It's been a long time coming," Mayor Denny said with a frown. "I've just been too nice."

He marched off, leaving Sarah and Mrs. Claus staring after him in shock.

Chapter Eleven

Meanwhile, Mr. Miller had just walked into his barn. Completely surprised to see the reindeer and sleigh, he stopped short.

"Someone's here," Comet whispered to the others.

Dancer turned and looked at the farmer. "Hey, who's this guy?"

"What on Earth!" Mr. Miller sputtered.

"Where did you reindeer come from?"

"Sorry, sir," Comet said. "We thought this barn was empty. We're from the North Pole." He started to introduce himself and the other reindeer.

But Mr. Miller didn't understand Comet's words. All he heard was a weird neighing sound.

"Quiet down," he scolded the reindeer.

Comet was surprised. "He can't understand us," he remarked. "He must not have any Christmas Spirit."

"But I thought Pineville had the most Christmas Spirit of all!" Dancer said.

Mr. Miller was no longer paying attention to their neighing. He was thinking very hard.

"Hmm," he said to himself. "It's

Christmastime. I bet I could sell these reindeer for a pretty penny!"

He rushed out of the barn, heading toward town.

A short while later, Mrs. Claus hurried into Mr. Miller's barn. "Oh, my loves!" she called to the reindeer. "You're not going to believe what has happened. At first I thought the whole town had a Christmas cold, but now it seems like some kind of terrible flu. We're going to need Santa's help!"

"It gets worse, Mrs. Claus," Comet said. "The owner of this barn said—"

Suddenly the barn door flew open. Mr. Miller was standing there with Pineville's sheriff.

"They're right in here, Sheriff," Mr. Miller said. Then he noticed Mrs. Claus. "Well, who's this?" he added.

"A trespasser?" Sheriff Andy asked.

"Hello, dear sirs," Mrs. Claus greeted them. "I'm Mrs. Cane. I was just letting my, er, reindeer rest in your barn."

"Be careful, Mrs. Claus," Comet said. "These guys are bad news. They've lost their Christmas Spirit."

Sheriff Andy looked disapprovingly at the reindeer. "That's illegal boarding of animals without knowledge or consent of the property owner."

"Yes, I suppose it is," Mrs. Claus admitted.

"We'd better talk about this down at the station," the sheriff said sternly.

"You're arresting me?!" Mrs. Claus exclaimed.

"Come with me please, ma'am," Sheriff Andy said.

"You can't arrest Mrs. Claus!" Comet cried.

But all the sheriff heard was neighing. He led Mrs. Claus out of the barn.

Soon Sheriff Andy was locking Mrs. Claus in a cell at the town jail. The heavy metal door slammed shut.

"Sheriff, you're a very nice young man and I don't want to break your laws," Mrs. Claus said, "but I can't stay here."

Sheriff Andy ignored her and walked away. He'd wasted enough time already!

Mrs. Claus sighed and leaned closer to

the bars of the cell. Her crystal glowed, and a little bit of magic dust swirled around the lock.

But it wasn't enough. The cell door stayed locked tight.

"Oh no," Mrs. Claus murmured. "My crystal's very, very weak."

She knew that wasn't a good sign. It meant Christmas Spirit was weakening all over the world, and the Great Christmas Icicle was being affected.

"Mrs. Cane?" a cheery voice said behind her. "Is that you?"

Mrs. Claus turned and saw the three Bright sisters at the back of the cell. "Oh dear!" she exclaimed. "Whatever could you three have done to end up in here?"

Dorothy Bright smiled sheepishly. "It

all happened so fast," she began.

With her sisters, she told Mrs. Claus the whole story. Every Christmas, the Brights brought cookies from Holman's Cookie Store to the children's floor at the local hospital. This year, when they'd gone to pick them up, the store was empty. The Brights had started filling a box with cookies as always, but then Mr. Holman had returned—and called the sheriff to come and arrest the sisters for stealing his cookies!

Mrs. Claus was glad that the Bright sisters still seemed to have their Christmas Spirit. But that wouldn't be enough to save Christmas. No, she had to do something to cure Pineville's terrible Christmas flu before it was too late.

But how could she while she was locked in jail?

Carter skated across the pond after the puck. The hockey game was in full swing, and it was a close one. All the boys were being very aggressive.

"Come on, pass it!" Mr. Miller shouted from the bank. He sounded so angry that Carter glanced over in surprise.

Suddenly a boy rammed into Emmett, sending him flying.

"Oof!" he grunted as he crashed into Carter, knocking him over.

Carter ended up spinning right into a snowbank. He jumped up and shoved Emmett.

"Don't push me!" Carter yelled.

Emmett frowned and pushed him. Carter pushed him back. He was so angry with his best friend that he couldn't stand it!

Just then Sarah arrived at the pond. She stared at her brother as he shoved his friend again. What was wrong with Carter these days? It seemed as if he was always in a bad mood!

Carter saw his sister watching him. Her shocked face made him feel guilty about getting so mad.

Mr. Miller stormed onto the ice. "That's it!" he shouted. "You kids are too much trouble. Get off my property! I never want to see you kids on my pond again!"

Emmett scowled and threw his stick

down. "You're the worst coach ever!" he yelled.

Sarah hurried over to Carter. "Are you okay?" she asked.

Carter rubbed his arm and nodded. What had just happened?

He and Sarah walked home in silence. When they got there, their father was just leaving. He told them that Mrs. Cane was in jail.

"She's been arrested—for reindeer trespassing, of all things," he said briskly. "Now I've got to go. It's really busy at work. People are suing each other like crazy!"

"But what about our family dinner?" Sarah asked.

"You're on your own," Mr. Reynolds

said. He hurried off without another word.

Sarah stared after him. "He's sick, Carter," she said. "He's got a Christmas cold. The only one who can help us is Mrs. Cane. And she's in jail! What do we do?"

Chapter Twelve

Jeb dragged a couple of dogs into the kennel room. It was crowded with cages.

"Another family dropped off their dogs," Jeb said, locking the newcomers in a cage. "Seems no one wants their pets anymore. Too much hassle. I can't say I blame them." He stomped out again.

Baxter was sitting near the Pups' cage. "I'm really sorry, guys," he said.

"Things are going from bad to terrible. I don't know what's gotten into him."

"He's lost his Christmas Spirit," Jingle told them.

"Baxter! You've really got to get us out of here," Noble said. "We need to find our crystal. We need to fix this—now!"

Baxter gulped. "I don't know, Pups," he said. "I'd get in big trouble."

"What's worse?" Noble asked him. "Big trouble or no Christmas?"

"Good point," Baxter said. "We'll just have to wait for the right opportunity. Hang tight."

The right opportunity came that night. Baxter hurried into the kennel room. "It's time, Pups," he said. "The coast is clear. And I've sniffed out your collar."

"I'm really impressed, Baxter," Charity said. "You're helping us save Christmas even though you might get in big trouble. That's, like, totally selfless!"

Baxter nosed open the Pups' cage. "Okay, let's get out of here!"

Baxter and the Pups sneaked out of the shelter and hurried down the street to a pawn shop. Baxter had discovered that Jeb had sold the crystal to the shop's owner.

The front door was locked, but Baxter led the way to the backyard. There was a doggy door there.

There was also a tough-looking bulldog sleeping in his doghouse, right next to the doggie door!

"That's Brutis," Baxter whispered. "He's the meanest dog in the entire county." He gulped. "Maybe we should forget about the crystal."

"We don't have any choice if we want to save Christmas," Noble reminded him.

Charity nodded. "He's asleep."

"We'll have to sneak by to get inside," Hope whispered.

Jingle was feeling nervous. "We'd better hurry up before I burst into song!" she whispered.

They tiptoed past the bulldog. Jingle started to hum, and Brutis stirred.

But Baxter and the Pups quickly ducked through the doggy door. Inside, the shop was crammed with stuff. How were they going to find the crystal in all that mess?

But Noble had an idea. "Look for the glow," he said.

They all searched the store. Baxter spotted something that was glowing faintly on top of a tall jewelry case.

"Guys—look!" he called.

The Pups rushed over. It was the crystal!

"How do we get up there?" Charity wondered.

Hope smiled. "Extreme ascents are my specialty," she replied.

She climbed up a mountain of boxes. Higher . . . higher . . . Finally she was high enough to grab the collar.

She had it!

"All right!" Baxter cheered. "Way to go, Hope!"

"Drop the crystal to me, sis," Noble added. Hope tossed the collar to him, and he slipped it on. "Be careful on the descent!" he called.

"Don't worry—the descent is my favorite part!" Hope called back. She took a running leap and jumped off the edge of the jewelry case.

"Whoo-hoo!" she yelled.

"No!" Charity yelped. "You'll wake up Brutis!"

It was too late. Hope landed on a pile of boxes with a loud *CRASH!* "That was radical!" she exclaimed.

A second later there was a bark from outside.

"Oh no . . ." Baxter said.

As the Pups hid, Baxter bravely stood his ground. Brutis stomped in and saw him.

"I was in the middle of a remarkable dream," Brutis grumbled. "I don't like being woken up. And I especially don't like being woken up by intruders. Baxter, are you trespassing?"

"Uh . . ." Baxter began.

Charity popped out of hiding. "Brutis, sir," she said. "It's all our fault. Don't hurt Baxter."

Brutis stared as the other Pups came out, too. "And who are you?"

"My name is Noble Paws," Noble said. "These are my sisters, Hope, Charity, and Jingle."

"We came down to Pineville on a mission," Hope explained. "But our plan backfired and now everyone in Pineville has a Christmas cold."

"Brutis," Baxter spoke up. "I know it's hard to believe, but it's true. Haven't you noticed your human behaving strangely?"

Brutis thought about that. "He has been pretty grouchy," he mused. "He's never gone this long without playing with me or giving me a treat. It's like he—"

"Lost his Christmas Spirit?" Charity finished for him.

"Yeah," Brutis agreed.

"If we don't get the crystal back and find Mrs. Claus, we fear Christmas will be gone forever," Charity told him.

"You mean no new chew toys on Christmas morning? And no Christmas cookie crumbs to lick up?" Brutis asked in shock. "Not on this dog's watch! Let's get you guys and the crystal out of here!"

He stood back and let Baxter and the Pups run out of the shop. They had the crystal. But they didn't have much time to find Mrs. Claus!

"You sure this is Pineville, Eddy?" Eli asked, looking around.

It was so late it was almost morning again. The ice cream truck had just landed in Pineville. The town was dark and gloomy.

Eddy nodded. "This is the place."

"Things have gone downhill fast," Eli said. "We have to locate Mrs. Claus immediately."

Eddy checked their locator. But the red blip that tracked Mrs. Claus's crystal had faded away.

"Oh, no!" Eddy cried. "I can't see the crystals anymore! The magic has become too weak."

"We have to find them the old-fashioned way," Eli realized, "using our instincts and intellect!"

Eddy nodded. "Mrs. Claus's last recorded position was the Reynolds house. Turn right here."

Chapter Thirteen

Sarah and Carter were stepping out the door to go to school when they saw an ice cream truck driving toward them. Christmas music poured out of its speakers.

"Ice cream!" Sarah exclaimed.

Carter blinked. "What's an ice cream truck doing here in December? At eight o'clock in the morning?"

"Hiya, kids!" Eli leaned out the window and waved. "We're looking for a jolly white-haired lady."

"I think you might be looking for Mrs. Cane," Sarah suggested.

"Mrs. Cane?" Eddy said. "As in candy cane?"

Sarah's eyes lit up. "Did that dog just talk?"

"What are you talking about?" Carter glanced from her to Eddy. "He just barked."

"Looks like we have a believer," Eli told Eddy.

"I'm sorry, mister," Carter said. "She's a little confused. All this Christmas stuff is going to her head."

"No I'm not, Carter," Sarah said. Then

she turned to Eli and Eddy again. "Mrs. Cane is in jail."

"*Jail?*" Eli cried. "We have to bust Mrs. Claus out of the clink! And we don't have much time!"

Inside the jail cell, Mrs. Claus and the Bright sisters were hard at work. They were trying to saw through the bars with three old nail files. But they weren't making much progress.

Suddenly, Eli's head popped into view in the window. "Hello, ladies," he said. "You haven't seen a Mrs. Claus around here, have you?"

Mrs. Claus gasped. "Eli? Thank heaven you're here!"

"Mrs. Claus!" Eli exclaimed. "I've got

Eddy with me, too." He peered past her. He couldn't see the main room, but he sure hoped Sarah and Carter were doing their job.

They'd all come up with a plan on the way over. The kids were supposed to distract Sheriff Andy, then handcuff his foot to his desk. That would give Eli and Eddy time to release Mrs. Claus.

"We're going to bust you out of here," Eli told her. "We don't have enough magic in our crystal, so we have to do it old school. Stand back everyone!"

CRASH!

Eli and Eddy pulled the wall down with the ice cream truck. In the other room, Sheriff Andy heard the commotion.

"*What* is going on?" he yelled.

He tried to stand up, but he couldn't. His foot was handcuffed to his desk! So he dragged the desk far enough to see into the cell area.

"We're sorry for the damage, Sheriff." Mrs. Claus gestured at the collapsed wall. "But there's something gone terribly wrong in Pineville and I needed to get out of that cell. Toodle-oo!" She waved.

"Remember to stay on the Nice list," Eli told the sheriff. "Come on, Eddy."

Mrs. Claus, Eli, Eddy, and the Bright sisters climbed out over the rubble of the wall. Sheriff Andy stared after them.

"Wait!" he called. "What about me?"

Mrs. Claus and the others met up with Carter and Sarah at the radio station.

"Eli, do we have any idea what's going on?" Mrs. Claus fretted.

"We haven't been able to figure it out," Eli said. "We thought you might know. It all happened so fast! It's as though someone wished for Christmas to go away—and *poof*! There it went."

"Wait a second," Carter said. "What did you just say?"

"Which part?" Eli asked.

"About the wish," Carter answered nervously.

Eli shrugged. "I was just saying, Christmas vanished so fast it's as if someone wished for it to go away. But who would make such a wish?"

Carter gulped. "I did," he realized. "I didn't mean to, but I did. I wished that

Christmas Spirit would go away. But I didn't think it would really happen."

"But who would grant that wish?" Mrs. Claus exclaimed. "Not any of us who have magic crystals!"

"There's something you should know," Eddy told her. "The Santa Pups stowed away on your sleigh, and my crystal is missing. We think they have it."

"The Pups must have granted Carter's wish," Eli said. "We have to reverse the wish and restore Christmas Spirit before it's too late!"

Carter took a deep breath and closed his eyes. "I wish Christmas Spirit would come back," he chanted.

Nothing happened.

Eli shook his head. "I wish it was that

easy," he told Carter. "The Santa Pups granted that wish, so they're the only ones who can reverse it."

"We need to find them," Eddy said. "And fast."

"In the meantime," Mrs. Claus added, "we have to find a way to stop the Christmas flu from spreading. We need to boost Spirit back up!"

Sarah looked over at the booth. There was a picture of her mother on the wall.

"I've got an idea," she said. "We can do what Mommy used to do."

"You mean the Christmas show?" Carter asked. He glanced at the others. "The show inspired the whole town. I know it used to inspire me."

"Great idea, Sarah," Mrs. Claus said.

"Eddy and Eli—go get the reindeer. They're in Mr. Miller's barn. The Santa Pups might be there." She turned to the Bright sisters. "Ladies, I want you to turn on every single radio in this town!"

Chapter Fourteen

The Santa Pups were still searching for Mrs. Claus so they could tell her what they had done. They decided to check Mr. Miller's barn. When they got there, they sneaked in through the back door.

"Noble, Hope, Charity, Jingle!" Comet exclaimed. "What are you Pups doing here?"

"And who is that scruffy elf dog?"

Dancer asked, staring at Baxter.

"I'm not an elf dog," Baxter said. "My name is Baxter and I'm from right here in Pineville."

"Baxter should be an honorary elf dog," Noble said. "He saved us from the pound. We're proud to call him a friend."

Dancer was confused. He still didn't understand where the Pups had come from. "You mean you didn't come down from the North Pole as part of a rescue party?" he asked.

"I'm afraid not," Jingle said.

"Then how did you get here?" Comet asked.

"It's a bit of a story," Noble said. "But right now, we need your help!"

Outside, Eli and Eddy were just driving up to the barn. The door was padlocked and there was a sign on it.

"'Reindeer for sale,'" Eli read. "This must be the place."

Normally, Eli and Eddy could use their crystals to get through the padlocked door. But that wouldn't work today. Luckily, Eli had another idea.

"Hang on," he warned Eddy.

And with that, Eli floored it. The tires spun, and the truck shot forward.

"Who needs crystals?" Eli shouted. *"Yeee-haaa!"*

CRASH! The truck smashed right through the barn door. Wood splintered everywhere.

The reindeer and the Pups jumped

out of the way of the truck. They were shocked—but very happy—to see the elves.

"Guys, we're saved!" Dancer cried. "And we've got ice cream! I hope they have sprinkles!"

"Eddy and Eli!" Hope exclaimed. "Boy, are we happy to see you!"

"I'm just going to come right out and admit it," Noble said. "We messed up and granted a bad wish."

"We'll get to that later," Eddy replied. "Right now we have to reverse that wish before it's too late."

At the radio station, Carter was trying to figure out how to work the sound board. Finally it lit up. Mrs. Claus clapped.

"It's showtime!" she said.

Carter spoke into the microphone. "Um, hello, Pineville," he said. "This is Carter . . ."

"And Sarah Reynolds," Sarah said, as she leaned toward the microphone. "Broadcasting live over 87.9 XMAS-FM, Pineville radio. This is the annual Christmas radio show."

"A tradition started by our grandfather over sixty years ago," Carter continued. "And made special by our mom, Michelle Reynolds. My sister and I are here to carry on that tradition."

At the same time, the Bright sisters were sneaking around town. Dorothy tiptoed into the courthouse, where Owen and

Mr. Kent were arguing over their lawsuit. She flipped on the radio, then tiptoed out again.

Blue eased in the back door of Holman's Cookie Store. She turned on the radio, then grabbed a few cookies on her way out.

Agnes burst into Mayor Denny's office. She switched on his radio—and the town hall loudspeaker—as he watched in surprise.

Meanwhile, the radio show was still going on. "I know you're all busy," Sarah told the listeners. "And some of you may be feeling a bit sad. But we need your help to bring Christmas Spirit back to our town."

Her voice poured out of the town speakers. People on the sidewalks stopped to listen.

Carter spoke next. "After my mom passed away I didn't feel like it was right to celebrate—so I did this. I don't know how exactly, but I did. I've made you all feel the way you do because I wished that Christmas Spirit would go away, and it did. It was like a flu—a Christmas flu. It spread from me, to the people I met, to the people they met."

In the courtroom, Mr. Reynolds heard him and looked up. "Carter?" he whispered.

"I know that if my mother was here," Carter continued, "she'd want us all to be happy and celebrate Christmas with the people we love, and to remember her by keeping the spirit of Christmas alive in Pineville."

At the radio station, Mr. Reynolds hurried into the booth. Carter looked up and saw him. Mr. Reynolds rushed over to hug his son.

"I love you, Dad," Carter said.

"I love you too, son."

Sarah took the microphone. "This is dedicated to my daddy, my brother, and my mommy," she told the listeners.

Then she began to sing a beautiful Christmas carol called "O Holy Night." Her lovely voice echoed out of speakers all over Pineville. People listened. They smiled. Tears came to their eyes and Christmas joy to their hearts.

Storekeepers began to repair their

lights and decorations, humming along with Sarah's song. Jeb released all the dogs in the shelter from their cages. Townsfolk gathered in front of the town hall and sang along.

And as Mrs. Claus sat and listened, her crystal began to glow. . . .

The dots on the Spirit Map were glowing, too. "Santa, look!" Ellis cried.

Santa Claus smiled as the gray dot over Pineville changed to orange. Other dots brightened and spread out from the town.

"It's spreading!" Santa Paws exclaimed. "The Christmas Spirit is spreading everywhere!"

Chapter Fifteen

The Christmas Spirit *was* spreading. By the time Sarah sang the final note of her song, Mrs. Claus's crystal was glowing brightly.

She smiled as the Santa Pups burst in to the radio station. Eli, Eddy, and Baxter were right behind them.

Mrs. Claus bent to greet the Pups.

"Oh, my darling Pups," she said. "I'm so glad you're safe."

"We're sorry, Mrs. Claus," Noble told her. "We thought we could prove that we were ready for crystals of our own."

Jingle nodded. "But instead we caused Christmas Spirit to go away in Pineville."

"I guess we still have a lot to learn," Charity agreed.

"Don't worry about that now," Mrs. Claus said. "We have to reverse the wish you granted in order to wipe out the Christmas flu for good."

Eddy nodded. "You've got the magic crystal," he told the Pups.

"You must grant the wish," Eli added.

All the Pups stared at Carter. He cleared his throat.

"I wish Pineville and the world a Merry Christmas forever!" he declared.

Magic dust floated out of the collar Noble was wearing. It swirled around everyone in the room.

Had they done it? Had they saved Christmas?

Everyone rushed to the window and looked out. Main Street was lit up with beautiful Christmas lights from one end to the other.

Mrs. Claus, the Pups, and their friends rushed out and joined the townspeople. They were hugging and apologizing to one another for their behavior over the past couple of days. Dogs were reuniting with their owners, who promised never to take them to the shelter again. Everyone joined in singing joyful holiday songs.

"Sorry I borrowed your magic crystal without asking, Eddy," Noble said, giving the crystal back.

"Don't worry, Noble," Eddy said. "Someday you'll have one of your very own."

Then the sleigh arrived to pick up Mrs. Claus and the Pups. It was time to say farewell.

"You shared your hearts and reminded everyone what Christmas is all about," Mrs. Claus told Carter and Sarah. "I came here to find one ambassador for the Santa Cause—and I found two!"

Carter and Sarah hugged her tightly. "Will we ever see you again?" Carter asked.

"Of course, dear," Mrs. Claus said. "You're my official ambassadors, and it's a very important role." She attached a sparkling pin to each of their coats. "It means you will embody the Christmas Spirit every day for the whole year. Can you do that?"

"Yes!" Carter and Sarah exclaimed happily.

"We'll never forget you," Sarah added.

"You won't have to," Mrs. Claus replied. "Because just like your mom, I'm going to be right there." She touched their hearts. "Forever."

"Merry Christmas, Pineville!" the Santa Pups cried as they piled into the sleigh.

They waved their paws goodbye, and the reindeer took off.

At the North Pole, everyone was happy and relieved.

"They did it!" Santa Paws said. "They saved Christmas!"

"I knew Mrs. Claus had everything under control." Santa Claus smiled. Then he let out a big belly laugh. "Ho, ho, ho!"

It was going to be a merry Christmas indeed.